LAST STOP ON THE Z TRAIN

*And other fantastic stories to read
while waiting for the train*

Stories by Jason Storbakken

Paintings by Pairoj Pichetmetakul

To Tzipi and Tzed

CONTENTS

FIRST STOP ON THE 1 TRAIN

The intergalactic architects designed a way in and a way out of every planet in the galaxy cluster. Earth was a challenge because its so-called *intelligent life* kept destroying itself with wars, genocides, and all sorts of violence. Thus, the architects needed to continue to create new portals to observe Earth.

Many great myths were formed around the location of these portals. The Garden of Eden, Lake Titicaca, and Mount Kailash were all once portals.

The newest portals were in New York City. The way in: first stop on the 1 train. The way out: last stop on the Z train.

Occlo and Capac loved to visit other planets, but they were only allowed to travel between the giant diamond supernova and the solar system with the two stars, which meant Earth was outside their perimeter.

Occlo and Capac were a bit mischievous and sometimes had a hard time following orders. Occlo loved Earth's juicy tube lip balm and Capac couldn't resist the pad thai, so they decided to take a quick trip to the little blue planet.

When they arrived on Earth at the South Ferry Station on the 1 train, they realized they had forgotten to bring their cloaking device. They had the shape of a human: a torso, two legs, two arms, and a head.

But there were differences.

For example, their skin was more like a tree's bark than a human's flesh and they had a lot more teeth than a human. They also wore royal attire, which simply looked like oversized clothes to an earthling.

Since they had neither proper disguises nor a voice translator – when they spoke all human ears heard is clacks, clicks, and high-pitched beeps – Occlo and Capac decided it would be best to make their way directly to the Z train.

Occlo and Capac did remember to bring pocket change with them, but their idea of pocket change was a huge stack of one-hundred dollar bills. As they hurriedly walked from the 1 train to the first stop on the Z line at Broad Street they tried to be discreet, but they soon got distracted.

They saw a homeless woman with a sign next to her hat soliciting donations. Occlo and Capac saw a few bills in the hat and decided to contribute. Little did they know they had given the lady thousands of dollars.

Occlo saw a stand selling assorted products, including lip balm, so she quickly purchased her beloved lip balm. And just before they arrived at the train station, Capac saw a Thai restaurant. He ordered the pad thai to go. Although it was a very quick visit, they were able to get what they most desired – lip balm and pad thai!

They got on a train and started toward their destination when they noticed a human girl child watching them.

"Act natural," said Capac to Occlo. But all the little girl could hear was a series of clacks, clicks, beeps, and slurps of pad thai.

"I am natural," said Occlo as she applied a generous amount of lip balm to her lips.

"Be careful you don't show all your rows of teeth."

"Oh yes, I forget that humans only have a top and bottom row. However do they get on?"

The little girl watched Occlo and Capac until she was whisked away by her adult at their stop.

As Occlo and Capac made their way closer to their portal home, they received a transmission from the mothership, "It is important that all intergalactic agents return to your home planet immediately. Great danger is lurking outside the galaxy." And with that Occlo and Capac hurried toward the last stop on the Z train.

PIZZA PUNCH

"**Y**ou're the height of fashion!" said Jenny.

She admired her mom but didn't often say as much. This New York trip promised to put her on the social map at her school back in Des Moines. It's not that Jenny didn't have friends, she just wasn't as popular as she pretended to be at home. She figured her parents thought she was popular, but in reality they knew she wasn't the coolest kid in school and they really just hoped she was *happy*.

Her parents didn't understand that happiness is merely a fleeting emotion, and it would prove more substantial if they aimed to instill in their children an abiding joy and sense of deep purpose.

"Your bronze Gucci bag looks fabulous against your sunshine yellow shirt." Mrs. Miller glowed in her daughter's adulation.

The Millers spent the morning on Canal Street in Chinatown buying imitation products. They knew the Rolexes and handbags were fake, but like many tourists they couldn't resist the allure of owning such popular products, even if they were fake.

Mr. Miller asked, "Jen, what do you think about our Rolexes?!"Mr. Miller and Timmy flashed the big chunk of bling strapped to their wrists. They all laughed.

It was a good morning. The trip had brought the family closer together than they had been in a long time.

"Hey dad," said Timmy, "How about a piece of pizza?"

"You just had two hot dogs and a bag of peanuts," said Mrs. Miller disapprovingly.

"But it's Ray's *Original* Pizza!" said Timmy.

Jenny said, "I've seen about six Ray's *Originals* today. There doesn't seem to be anything original about it, except for your capacity to eat!"

"I wasn't talking to you," snarled Timmy. "How about it, dad?"

"Ok, but let's get it to go. I want to stay on our itinerary."

Mr. Miller and Timmy each got a slice of pepperoni. Mrs. Miller and Jenny didn't want a slice. They were happy with their handbags.

The Millers went into the subway to make their way to the next stop. Mr. and Mrs. Miller buried themselves in the subway map while Jenny began to provoke Timmy.

"You better slow down on eating, big boy," taunted Jenny. Timmy was self-conscious of his weight. He tried to ignore her and eat his slice in peace. "You got some good birthing hips," she continued.

Mr. Miller laughed and Timmy lost it. Timmy tried to shove Jenny.

Mrs. Miller shouted, "Knock it off. I don't want to have to scrape you two off the tracks."

Timmy sneered at Jenny, "Your nasty attitude is why you don't have any friends!"

He knew just what to say to hurt her.

She pushed him hard right in the gut. He keeled over and his pizza went flying. He didn't know what hurt more, the shove to the gut or the lost slice of pizza.

"If you don't get it together we'll go straight back to the hotel," said Mr. Miller. A train was coming but not in the direction they were going. In their confusion they got on the wrong train going in the wrong direction.

* * *

RAT PACK

"**G**o ahead. I dare ya."

"Yeah. You're a lot of talk, Ivar. Let's see if you really are descended from Vikings."

Tweaks and Bernie pushed Ivar who proudly and often claimed to be a Norwegian rat and thus descended from the fierce rats that once sailed on Viking ships.

"I don't need to prove a thing. Why don't you do it, Bernadette?"

"I told you. You can call me Bernie or Berns, but do not call me Bernadette."

"Ok, Berns. You think you're so street smart. You got all the grit. You do it!"

Bernie didn't have any pretenses. She was proud to be a regular ol' New York City sewer rat.

"Well," said Bernie, "if you're not gonna do it and I'm not gonna do it. How about you, Tweaks?"

Tweaks was fairly new to the pack. He escaped from a lab and was considered a bit cuckoo by Ivar and Bernie. But they liked him and respected him.

"F-f-fine," stammered Tweaks, a side effect of the experiments they ran on him in the laboratory. "I'll d-d-do it."

Ivar, Bernie and Tweaks looked through the grate. There was a perfect slice of pepperoni pizza on the platform floor. It was just waiting for them to take it. The only problem was that it was rush hour and they needed to get it before sanitation swept it up and threw it away.

Tweaks, in a fit of fury, made a mad dash toward the slice of pizza pie. People parted. Children screamed. An old woman nearly fainted and her husband fell over backward when he tried to swat Tweaks with his cane. A businessman shrieked and jumped on top of the bench. Berns and Ivar had never heard such a shrill in all their life. Everyone was screaming and jumping and falling over.

Tweaks grabbed the slice of pie, cheese still gooey. The weight of the pizza made him slow. But he was determined. He dragged that pizza slice back to the grate and disappeared from the sight of the humans.

"Good rat, Tweaks, good rat!" said Ivar.

"You the rat! You the rat!" shouted Bernie.

❋ ❋ ❋

THE CASE OF THE MYSTERY LIQUID

Ｎew Yorkers aren't afraid of much, but they do have a few fears. Recently, there was a poll on Twitter that ranked the top fears of New Yorkers. Here are the top five.

1. Pushed onto subway tracks.
2. Falling through a sidewalk grate.
3. Bedbugs.
4. Toilet rat.
5. Subway mystery liquid.

Subway mystery liquid – that drip-dropping mysterious fluid that falls from the subway ceiling, settles on the platform, and drips onto the track or dissipates into the subway air. There was a never ceasing drip of this liquid at the 4 train stop at 125th Street.

Most people knew to steer clear of the drip, but Ezzie Hogan had just moved to Harlem from the Bronx. One day while she was waiting for the train to visit friends in her old neighborhood she happened to be standing directly under the spot where the mystery liquid falls. And a drop of that strange goo fell onto page 52 of her favorite book, *The House on Mango Street.* The liquid landed in the center of the page where it read:

"Engine, engine number nine,

running down Chicago line.

If the train runs off the track

do you want your money back?"

Ezzie examined her book. The word *Chicago* was covered by the murky goo. Ezzie did not know where the drop came from so she looked around and just as she looked up a next drop fell from the subway ceiling directly toward Ezzie's face.

Julio, a boy a few years younger than Ezzie, grabbed her by the sleeve and pulled her from the falling droplet of goo.

"Get your hands off me," insisted Ezzie.

"I just saved your life," said Julio. He pointed to

where Ezzie had been standing and she saw a very small puddle of green goo.

"Thank you," she said reluctantly.

"My name is Julio. Julio Colon. I'm an amateur detective and I'm currently on the case of the mystery liquid."

Ezzie laughed.

"You might laugh," said Julio, "but a single drop of that mystery liquid landed on mi abuela's eyebrows and now she has no eyebrows. Would you like to help me?"

Ezzie was intrigued. She decided to delay her trip to her old neighborhood and help crack the case.

He told her to stand back and observe the mystery liquid. It slowly dripped. Harlem natives knew to avoid the mystery liquid. It was uneventful until a family of lost tourists arrived on the platform and stood directly beneath the dripping goo.

Ezzie and Julio observed.

Julio opened his writing pad and described the family, the location where they stood, and the frequency of the drips (*Every 8 seconds.*).

The goo dripped directly onto the father's baseball cap as he read the subway map. The father readjusted and a drop of goo landed on the map. The curious father looked around for the source of the mystery liquid and just as he looked up toward the ceiling, mouth wide open, a drop of goo dripped directly into his mouth.

"Argh!" the father gurgle-shouted.

"What's wrong," asked Mrs. Miller.

Noticing the goo that settled on his cap, he shook

it off and inadvertently sprayed the goo all over his family's brightly colored shirts. The family erupted into a frantic mess.

"I think we've seen enough. Let's go to mi abuela's apartment for churros," said Julio.

"How can you think about eating at a time like this?" said Ezzie. "We need to question your abuela about her missing eyebrows and the mystery liquid."

When they entered his abuela's apartment they saw her sitting at the kitchen table, drinking Café Bustelo, and looking into a magnifying mirror as she carefully plucked her eyebrows.

"What are you doing?" asked Julio.

"Making myself presentable," said abuela. "Mr. Santiago from 1A has asked me to join him for dinner this evening."

"It looks like the mystery liquid has nothing to do with your abuela's missing eyebrows," said Ezzie.

"No. But we did crack the case," said Julio as he opened his notebook and scratched out where he had written, *The Case of the Mystery Liquid.* In its place he wrote, *The Case of the Disappearing Eyebrows.* In all caps next to it he wrote: **CASE CLOSED**.

❋ ❋ ❋

TITI

Titi lived in an abandoned nursing home in the South Bronx. She was old enough to live in an actual nursing home with nurses and other residents her age. But she couldn't afford to live in one of those and she refused to live in a shelter or state-run facility.

She wasn't alone in the abandoned nursing home.

The home had four floors.

The first floor's occupants were freegans. They were anti-capitalist and sought to help the environment by reducing waste. They salvaged discarded food and other items. They believed housing should be free and so they chose to live in the abandoned nursing home. They dumpster-dove to get most of their food, furnishings, and other items, and did their best to avoid the use of money.

The second floor served as the clubhouse for a group of young people who some city residents might call a street gang. They called themselves the Red Tigers.

The third floor once housed the severely mentally ill and now it housed a motley crew of people who all seemed to be hiding from something. They seldom made eye contact with those they didn't know well. The newer members of their crew were expected to panhandle to get money for the group.

Titi lived alone on the fourth floor. The fourth floor was abandoned because there was extensive fire damage caused by an arsonist a few years earlier. Titi had cleaned one of the rooms and made her home there.

But she was mindful that she lived on an abandoned floor of an abandoned nursing home. She often felt lonely.

Prior to living in the nursing home she rode the 5 train, but she couldn't make a home on the train.

Titi treated all the occupants of the abandoned nursing home with warmth and welcome. But inside she felt sad and alone. Everyone was glad that Titi lived among them. Other residents occasionally visited her and told her their hopes and struggles. Titi listened deeply and held all their dreams and woes. She only offered advice when asked. She was like a distant aunty to many of them. But they didn't always know how to show their appreciation for her.

One day they decided to throw her a party. The freegans had foraged pastries and party hats. Occupants of the third floor panhandled enough money to buy a stack of pizza pies, but most of the third floor residents chose not to attend. And the Red Tigers decorated the clubhouse to host the party. The Red Tigers were most eager to celebrate Titi because they had felt most loved and cared for by her.

Ricky, a member of the Red Tigers, went to Titi's floor to invite her to a surprise party in her honor. When he arrived at her room she was motionless and her body was stiff. Life had left her body. Ricky returned to the clubhouse. They ate the pizza, but didn't wear the party hats.

⁂ ⁂ ⁂

SWITCHEROO ON THE 6

A parent has no greater fear than losing a child, especially in New York City's labyrinthine subway system. On the bustling 6 train platform at rush hour two boys who did not know each other stood by their adults and waited for the train. One boy was waiting for the uptown express and the other boy was waiting for the downtown local. A signboard with the MTA map stood between them. The boys caught sight of one another and were suprised that their physical appearance was identical.

They talked while their adults were oblivious. The uptown boy was with his nanny. He was returning from Beacon Grace Academy to the hotel penthouse where he lived with his mother and her investment banker husband. The downtown boy was with his mom. He was returning from PS43 to the rent-controlled apartment where he lived with his parents, big sister, and twin toddler siblings Nathalie and Nathan.

The uptown boy said to the downtown boy, "Let's trade lives for the weekend." They had little time to decide because the trains were approaching. They exchanged important information – names of family members, friends, etc. – and they quickly traded coats and hats and backpacks. The adults didn't notice a thing.

The uptown boy went downtown. The apartment was small, but cozy. The big sister helped him with his homework. She was surprised by how much his math skills had seemed to improve so quickly.

Next, the children, including the twin toddlers, played together. The toddlers were confused their *big brother* didn't know their normal games and wasn't as much fun as usual.

When the father came home he helped the mother prepare a casserole. It wasn't as decadent as the meals the boy was accustomed to eating, but it was tasty. Dinner at the downtown boy's home was a raucous, joyful event. After dinner the dad read a chapter from *The Horse and His Boy*, prayed, and both parents kissed each child and tucked them in to bed.

As the children slept, the parents discussed their son's peculiar behavior. They were concerned about him, but figured he must simply be under the weather.

The downtown boy went uptown. He explored the huge and ornately decorated penthouse. It somehow felt empty to the downtown boy who was accustomed to the lovely raucous of his home life.

The nanny handed him over to a private tutor. The tutor was frustrated by the boy's seemingly diminished math skills but impressed by his improved creative writing ability.

After homework, he explored the game room, rooftop swimming pool, and indoor jungle gym. His mother was surprised by her son's renewed interest in these activities.

At dinner he ate with his mother. *Sit proper,* said the boy's mother as a chef served chicken cordon bleu. For dessert, they ate crème brulee.

The mother's investment banker husband returned home after dinner. He took his meal in the parlor where he watched Sports Center on the television. The mother put the boy to bed, kissed him, and said good night.

On Monday, after their whirlwind weekend, the boys met again at the subway station near the signboard where they first met. Both boys were with their mothers. They exchanged coats and hats and backpacks. As the boys talked and laughed together, the mothers noticed each other.

"Lisa!?" the downtown mother said.

"Lora!?" exclaimed the uptown mother.

Lisa and Lora were fraternal twins, raised in midtown, who had not seen each other since before their boys were born. They embraced and promised to meet together soon for coffee or bellinis.

✳ ✳ ✳

MARCOS MEETS THE MILLERS

The Miller family had been in New York City for only one day when they met Marcos.

The Millers were from Iowa. Their t-shirts were each a different primary color. Mr. Miller wore blue, Mrs. Miller wore yellow, Timmy wore green, and Jenny wore red. New Yorkers like dark colors, which made the Millers stand out. The Millers also spoke loudly, likely because they were used to open spaces with few people.

They were on their way to visit Times Square. Earlier in the day they visited Ground Zero. But somehow they got turned around and ended up in Queens.

A young man named Marcos gave them directions to Times Square. "Just hop on the 7 and it'll take you directly to Times Square," Marcos told the Millers.

Marcos was a food delivery person for a Spanish deli. He enjoyed delivering habichuelas, pernil, chicharrones, and other delicious food to hungry people, but he hoped to one day open his own Mexican restaurant where he could serve tacos, tamales, and flautas.

He was supposed to work later in the day, but he received a call from his wife, Alma, saying she was about to give birth. Their first child was on her way! They had decided to name their baby Teresa after Marcos' favorite titi.

After giving the Miller family directions, Marcos asked Mr. Miller for a swipe. Since Marcos hadn't worked that day, he didn't have money for a subway fare.

Mr. Miller was a fine man but he and his wife had to save a long time to save for this trip. Plus, before leaving for their New York City vacation, several neighbors and coworkers warned Mr. Miller about the dangers of New York City and the con artists and grifters who wait for tourists who make an easy mark. Marcos seemed like a nice guy, but Mr. Miller wasn't taking any chances.

The Millers rushed through the turnstile one-by-one in their primary color t-shirts as Mr. Miller swiped them each through. Mr. Miller went through last. He refused to look at Marcos.

The Millers made their way to the train platform just as Marcos had instructed.

Marcos had enough. He needed to get to the hospital to be with Alma. Against his better judgment he jumped the turnstile.

Transit police were lurking around the corner and seized upon him immediately. They asked for his ID, which he didn't have. If he had an ID he would only receive a summons of about $50, but if he had that kind of money he would have bought a metrocard.

Marcos was handcuffed and taken to booking where he'd be processed and placed in jail until his court date, which could take several days.

Two thoughts raced through Marcos' head.

First, he thought of his cousin Julio who jumped a turnstile a few years back and didn't have an ID.

When Julio went before the judge he was transferred to an immigration detention center and eventually deported.

Marcos' second thought was his family. *Alma and Teresa. Who would provide for them? Who would love them the way he could? How would they make it?*

As the Millers made their way to the platform, Timmy asked his dad, "What do you think he did?"

"Well, son, he must be some sort of criminal or gang member. The police don't arrest a person unless they did something wrong."

Jason Storbakken

THE ARTIST'S GIFT

The artist doodled in his drawing pad every day. He had a gift. Everything he drew came true. For example, a couple was arguing and he drew them smiling and holding hands. As soon as he gave them his drawing the couple smiled at each other and held hands.

Another time he saw a homeless woman sleeping on the train. He drew her sitting upright as if on a throne. And in the drawing he placed before her a crown filled with money. He placed the drawing inside a hat next to her feet. People saw the drawing and dropped change and bills into the hat. When the woman awoke, she smiled with surprise to see her hat filled with money, but she seemed even happier to see the drawing portraying her with dignity and regality.

Another time the artist witnessed a birthday boy accidentally let loose all of his birthday balloons. The artist drew a clown with a big red nose and a rainbow wig accompanied by a dancing poodle in a tutu. The artist took the drawing, folded it into a paper airplane, and just as he flew it toward the birthday boy, the clown and dancing poodle entered their train car from the previous car. It was the best surprise the birthday boy could have imagined.

The artist preferred to ride the A train. It provided plenty of opportunity for inspiration and participation in the human experience. At 31 miles, the A train is the longest subway line in New York City. He rode the A through Brooklyn, Queens and Manhattan.

Most days he tried to positively contribute to society, but some days he was moody and his doodles were unkind.

One day a very old woman boarded the train. There were no seats available. And no one offered her a seat. The artist could have chosen to draw passengers offering her a seat. He could even have drawn a plush recliner for her to sit on. Instead, he drew a big, fat rat running across the laps of the passengers who did not offer the lady a seat.

Sometimes he drew things of which he was unaware as if he were an extension of his drawing pad rather than the drawing pad serving as an extension of the artist.

One day as the train was stuck underground between Fulton Street in Manhattan and High Street in Brooklyn, the artist began to draw the subway tunnel as a wormhole from another world.

Unbeknownst to the artist, a one-eyed intergalactic marauder by the name of General Isab entered our world through the wormhole. She disguised herself and lived in the subway system.

She was on a reconnaissance mission to see if

Earth should be left alone, enslaved, or destroyed. The artist did not know that he had opened a portal from another world. Neither did he know that Earth's judgment was ushered in by a simple doodle.

* * *

"I'M NOT STARING.
I'M SMELLING."

"**S**top staring, Irene," I hear my mother say. I'm not staring. I'm smelling. My parents and teachers think that I'm easily distracted, but really I just find a great many things interesting. I see the special and unique but also strange and peculiar quality in many things.

That smell. The man sitting across from me – I think he's a man – is eating noodles. Looks and kinda smells like pad thai. I never like the smell of other people's food on the subway. But it's not even this guy's food that is peculiar. He doesn't look quite right. His legs, if you can call them that, look like skinny tree trunks. They're covered by big baggy pants, but I see small stems with buds branching at the ankle. Also his hair – you might not believe me, but it's true – his hair is like liquid.

There's a lady just like him sitting next to him. I assume she's a lady because she's applying what looks to be lip gloss. But when she opens her mouth it looks like she has not one but two extra rows of teeth. Between him taking slurps of noodles and her applying lip balm, I can hear them talking to each other in clicks and clacks and high pitch beeps.

People think I'm easily distracted but no one else on this entire train even notices these two intergalactic aliens. Yes, I'm pretty sure they are not from this planet. And no one even notices. Everyone is glued to their phones and iPads and other technology. Well, this intergalactic couple seems friendly enough. They kinda seem like tourists. It's really true that every culture is represented in New York City. And now we've got aliens. My mom just nudged me. It's our stop.

* * *

I LOVE MUSIC

Hip Hop Bob loved hip hop so much that he never wore headphones. Instead he carried a large speaker so that he could share with the world the fat beats and tight rhymes of his favorite hip hop artists. Hip Hop Bob was an old school purist who only played KRS-One, Public Enemy, Eric B and Rakim, and nothing later than LL Cool J's *Mama Said Knock You Out.*

One day while waiting for the C train at the Hoyt-Schermerhorn stop – the same station where Michael Jackson filmed the music video for *Bad*– Salsa Sam walked up to Hip Hop Bob and said angrily, "Why don't you play something else? Why don't you play some real music?" Hip Hop Bob glared at Salsa Sam and said in a tough tone, "It's your lucky day. I'm taking requests."

Salsa Sam was flabbergasted. He never heard of Hip Hop Bob taking requests. Salsa Sam said sheepishly, "My favorite song is *Rebelion*." Hip Hop Bob queued it up and hit play. The whole station was filled with the pit pat of congas and the triumph of the horn section.

Salsa Sam looked at his sister Matilda and said, "Let's dance!"

Matilda said, "No salsa for me. I like Heavy Metal." She then looked at Hip Hop Bob and said, "Please play *Iron Man!*"

But before Hip Hop Bob could queue up *Iron Man*, his hip hop crew appeared on the scene. Hip Hop Harry, the leader of the crew, looked at Hip Hop Bob, and asked, "Why are you playing *this* music?" Are you joining the salsa squad? You know we *only* play hip hop."

At that moment Cheeto, who always wore orange and spoke in a high-pitched fast pace, said, "Look! I only roll with you guys because I like you. I don't like hip hop. I don't like salsa. I love pop music." Everyone looked at Cheeto in disbelief, but he continued to speak his truth. "I once had Bieber fever and was afraid to tell you guys because of what you might say."

Salsa Sam spoke up, "I admit that I too had a case of Bieber fever."

Hip Hop Harry in a fit of indignation loudly proclaimed, "Hip Hop reigns supreme."

Salsa Sam in an act of defiance screamed, "Salsa siempre.

Emotions were escalating. Feelings were about to get hurt. At that moment Cool Mo walked into the heart of the group. He removed his ear buds and asked, "What's happening!" At that everyone tried to make their case as to why their preferred music genre is the best. In the midst of the confusion, Cool Mo asked Hip Hop Bob to plug his music into his speaker. The joyful sounds of the O'Jays *I Love Music* filled the station. The solo bongo drum intro drew everyone in and the wisdom of the lyrics opened their minds and softened their hearts:

"I love music

Any kind of music

I love music, just as

Long as it's grooving."

No one could resist the deep truth of the O'Jays.

The platform became a dance party where Bob, Sam, Matilda, Harry, Cheeto, and Cool Moe dug the deep groove.

* * *

SUBWAY ON ANOTHER WORLD

Most people ignored Elisabeth. She was well into her 80s and had lived at the Columbus Circle station for nearly a year. She was missing an eye. It wasn't that she was simply blind in one eye, which was true, but she actually had one complete eyeball missing. Sometimes she'd open wide her eyelid between her thumb and pointer finger to give a surprise to the children making their way to school.

Elisabeth was a heavy woman and not very mobile. She was fond to let people know that when she was younger she had a striking figure and she was confident she still had that figure *hidden away in there somewhere*. A person once asked Elizabeth where she went to the bathroom since she'd never seen her leave the subway. Elizabeth laughed and pointed over the platform, but in her heart she felt the question was inappropriate and too personal.

Elisabeth had one friend. Elisabeth met Irene on her first day of first grade. At first Irene always wanted to look into Elisabeth's eyehole to see if she could see her brain. Then she became deeply interested in Elisabeth's pocket watch. It was glorious and gold and oh so beautiful and Elisabeth always kept the correct time.

Irene's mom took her to school most days. She found Elisabeth to be a bit eccentric, but not crazy. And she occasionally gave her a dollar to buy a coffee or bag of peanuts. Only once did Irene's mom seem concerned about a story Elisabeth told Irene. But she didn't pull her away nor did she pull herself away once she started her story.

"I'm not really from Brooklyn," Elisabeth confided. "I'm from another world altogether."

"Is it far away?" asked Irene.

"Yes and no. If you used the best and fastest spaceship that humans could build and traveled for an entire lifetime you wouldn't even get close. But if you used technology from my world you could simply bend time and space and be there in a flash."

"Do you have subways in your world?"

"Oh yes and you would consider them weird and wonderful. They are not metal machines that run by electricity. They are giant worms that travel through underground tunnels. They have eight stomachs and each of them opens up to welcome passengers."

"Do you have to buy a metrocard?"

"Well, it's what you might call a symbiotic relationship. While you travel inside these giant worms the seats and poles that passengers hold are kind of like a digestive system. It absorbs nutrients and minerals from the bodies of the passengers. When you exit these *subways* you are pooped out or vomited at your station. But no one thinks it strange because everyone does it."

"For real?" asked Irene.

"So real," answered Elisabeth.

"Well, I hear your train coming, Irene. And today I plan to return to my world."

"How?"

"My timepiece."

To Elisabeth's surprise, Irene hugged her. They parted. Irene went to school. And Elisabeth returned to her world.

* * *

SUSPICIOUS PACKAGE

Rashi was on his way to school when he saw a suspicious package under the bench where he sat. It was the first time he ever rode alone on the subway. He felt especially brave but also a little nervous.

The package drew his attention. He tried to ignore it but the shiny red wrapping paper and beautifully tied golden bow seemed to call to him. He moved one seat closer to the package.

He knew what the signs said: "See something, say something." And he often heard the conductor's announcement: "If you see a suspicious package, alert an MTA employee."

This definitely qualifies as a suspicious package, thought Rashi. Yet he drew closer to it. He kicked it gently and the top of the package popped open like a jack-in-the-box. He looked inside and saw a handwritten note on fancy stationary. He carefully took the note and read it:

My Dear Rashi,

You are formally summoned to attend a great banquet in your honor. The banquet is to be held in the World Below. Follow the arrow on the reverse side of this summons and you will find your way to where you belong.

Signed,

Malodor

Rashi was troubled. *Why is my name written on this invitation? Isn't a summons an order? Who is Malodor?*

He looked at the reverse side of the note and saw a blinking arrow that seemed to point in the direction he was expected to go. It led him to the edge of the platform to a small ladder.

He remembered his mom's words, *If you go on the track you won't come back.* He assumed she had meant that if he went on the track he might be electrocuted by the third rail or maybe he'd be hit and killed by a train. And yet he was compelled to follow the arrow. He was led into the darkness of the subway.

Peculiar but friendly creatures that glowed in the dark lit his way. He followed the arrow to a door. The glowing creatures also pointed toward the door. He turned the handle and it opened.

When the door opened a gentle wind, like a fresh breath, washed over him.

Inside was a great hall. In the center was a long dining table covered with all types of delicious foods, fruits, and desserts. Many strange and fantastic guests dressed in royal clothes sat around the table. At one head of the table sat Malodor. She was dressed in layers of multi-colored robes and she wore an elaborate crown that looked like deer antlers. Across from Malodor was an empty seat reserved for Rashi.

Rashi took his seat and immediately joined the banquet.

Malodor approached Rashi and breathed on him. And in that breath he learned the secrets and mysteries of the World Below and how it was discovered by Above Grounders when they were digging subway tunnels. He learned how World Belowers and Above Grounders were once friends but conflict arose when the princess of the World Below married a commoner from Above Ground. The World Belowers retreated deeper into the earth and hid from the Above Grounders.

Malodor breathed on Rashi again and Rashi only saw the dark, dirty subway with rats scurrying in shadows. Malodor said, "We mask the beauty of the World Below by breathing magic on Above Grounders." Rashi asked to return to the banquet. Malodor again breathed on him and he found himself in the middle of the banquet as if he never left.

Malodor continued, "I always warned my daughter, the princess, *If you go on the track you won't come back*. And because she chose to live Above Ground she relinquished her right to the throne. We have been waiting for her child who is the heir of the Kingdom of the World Below to arrive and take his rightful seat on the throne."

Rashi then realized that he was sitting on the royal throne of which Malodor spoke.

"Prince Rashi, you now have a choice to make," said Malodor. "Stay here and reign over your Kingdom but never return to the Above Ground. Or return Above Ground and I will breathe on you and you will forget this world, never to return."

Rashi considered his options. He knew he'd miss his parents and neighborhood, and school and friends. But he was enticed by the magic he was able to wield in the World Below. He thought for a long time and then made his final decision.

Many years passed. Rashi married and had a child. And as his grandmother told his mother, and his mother told him, so he too told his child, "If you go on the track you won't come back."

* * *

FAIRX VS. DWARTS

For generations a war waged late at night when the trains slowed and fewer passengers traveled. The fairx and dwarts battled hard against each other. The fairx, a tiny little winged people, had magic like a fairy, but were mischievous like a pixie. And dwarts were crafty like dwarfs but nasty spirited like trolls. Neither the fairx or dwarts were the most pleasant among the mystical creatures that inhabit the subway.

While the MTA employs custodians to keep the subways clean, it is known by members of the custodians' guild that each night when there is the least amount of movement in the subway system, the fairx appear and remove litter from the tracks and platforms. The fairx also remove inappropriate graffiti and, in turn, create good graffiti to cover inappropriate subway ads. The dwarts preferred a gritty underground and sought to undo the fairx' magic in the subway. They liked grime, favored inappropriate graffiti, and reveled in the wonderment of mystery liquid.

The height of the fairx-dwart war took place in the 1970s and '80s. Most people think that the graffiti artists in this era chose to remain anonymous because they didn't want to get arrested, but the truth is that the fairx and dwarts created much of this graffiti in the heat of many battles. As Lady Pink, the Rolling Thunder Writers, Kel and other famous graffiti artists bombed subway cars in the '70s and '80s, so did the fairx and dwarts. In fact, Fairx invented bubble style lettering and the dwarts were the first to write wildstyle.

The end of the war began when the dwarts captured the fairx king. The battles ceased, but plotting and conspiring increased. After several long seasons the fairx queen devised a plan to rescue her king and finally win the war. She met with her advisers and explained that she would pretend to surrender but at the last minute spring a surprise attack and capture the entire dwart royal house. The advisers told their generals of the plans and they moved forward. The fairx sent a message to the dwarts by spray-painting on subway cars: *Fairx to surrender in exchange for king.*

A meeting was arranged for the fairx queen to surrender. Both royals houses made their way to the rendezvous point on the F line at Coney Island.

Little did the royal houses of fairx and dwart know that the fairx prince and dwart princess had become great friends, and they were making their own plan to end the war.

The fairx queen approached the dwart armed guards to surrender, but her archers were hiding, ready to shoot their arrows into the hearts of their enemies. Just as both parties approached each other an unscheduled train came barreling down the track. And in the conductor's car sat the fairx prince and dwart princess. Their plan was naïve but borne of friendship and the desire for reconciliation.

They planned to arrive with a party train carrying cake, a sound system, and party hats. But they were ill-equipped to drive the hijacked train.

They lost control.

The train was barreling toward the assembly of fairx and dwarts. It looked as if all was doomed until the dwarts and fairx put aside their conflict and focused all their magic on stopping the train. Their magic was strong enough to slow it down, but not stop it completely.

The fairx king managed to break free of his shackles and added a last bit of glitter magic.

But the glitter magic became a glitter bomb.

There was smoke and crying and glitter everywhere. Fairx and dwarts scrambled to make sure their loved ones were safe.

When the smoke cleared and glitter settled, the fairx prince and dwart princess emerged. The princess placed an album on the turntable and dropped some insanely beautiful beats.

Their plan failed and yet their mission was a success.

Dwarts and fairx danced together. They wore party hats and laughed, and ate cake.

The fairx and the dwarts were reconciled so deeply that in the next generation, there was a new people group – the dwarx!

Unfortunately, it didn't take long for a new conflict to arise when a fraction insisted that they not be called dwarx, but instead be called by another name, the fairts! But the story of the outlandish fairts will have to wait for another day.

❋ ❋ ❋

THE GHOST TRAIN OF BEDFORD AND NOSTRAND

W e were standing on the subway platform when an empty train pulled into the track. Its lights were on but it had no passengers and it appeared that there was no train operator in the engine.

I looked at my children. My son, a first grader, and daughter, a third grader, had their backpacks on. They were ready for school. We hoped to catch the 7:31 a.m. train so that they might make the Early Bird program.

When I saw the empty train pull in I knew we would be late. I asked them, "Do you think you can handle hearing the true story of the ghost train of Bedford and Nostrand?"

"Of course we can!"

"Are you sure?"

They nodded their head in agreement.

A long time ago in the early days of the age of locomotion there were two best friends. The boy was named Bedford and the girl was named Nostrand. They often adventured together through the forests and creeks of Brooklyn. In those days Brooklyn was less developed. There were trees and even some forest. Bedford and Nostrand's favorite place to go was the railroad yard to watch the laborers build trains and tracks.

One day Bedford said to Nostrand, "Let's sneak out tonight and explore the train yard when the workers are away."

"That sounds fun but scary," said Nostrand.

That night they snuck down to the train yard in the dark of night. There were no workers around. A glorious new train caught their eye.

"Let's check it out," said Nostrand.

They climbed into the train. Bedford pushed a

lever in the engineer's car. The train started to move. It went faster and faster. The train entered a tunnel and continued to increase in speed. The track was not yet finished. At full speed they crashed into a wall. Bedford and Nostrand perished that night.

I paused to look at my children. Another man on the platform seemed to be smiling with amusement as I told my children this tale, but I knew in my heart of hearts that this tale was not a tale for mere amusement, but in fact is the tale of Bedford and Nostrand. The empty train car with lights on but no passengers slowly pulled away.

I continued, "Today the ghost train rides the G line. And it was at this station, Bedford and Nostrand, where those two young people perished. Sometimes you can still see them in the engineer's car of the ghost train. On rare occasions, they can be seen on the opposite platform."

My children looked at me wearily. "What were they wearing the night they perished?" asked my third grader.

"It is said that Bedford wore brown slacks and a beige cotton shirt. Nostrand wore a yellow dress and a brown backpack. And they are said to always be seen looking longingly into each other's eyes as if they are grieving their decision to sneak out that horrible night."

My third-grader then noticed across the platform two young people that matched that exact description. She could not speak but merely pointed. In a grave voice my first-grader said ominously, "I think we have been haunted this day."

TIME TRAVEL ON THE MTA

D r. Kalinga had worked on practical theories of astrophysics his entire career, but his true passion was time travel. He held doctorates in three fields: physics, mechanical engineering, and cultural anthropology. Dr. Kalinga's wife had passed away two short years ago and he was left the task to care for his 11 year old daughter, Gigi, and 6 year old son, Yolo.

The Kalinga family's morning started with challenges – they overslept because they stayed up late watching a documentary on ancient Kemet, their breakfast porridge burned to the bottom of the pot, and Dr. Kalinga had a hard time finding his favorite bow tie.

Dr. Kalinga had an important meeting where he

was scheduled to present his newest theory to a group of investors who could potentially fund his research. Inside his briefcase he had more than a theory – he carried a container filled with chronoplasm that if properly deployed might, just might, transform an object regardless of size into a time travel machine.

Dr. Kalinga's children were both carrying heavy backpacks – it was library day and they had many books to return. Gigi and Yolo were both advanced readers for their age. Yolo was returning the Wild Robot, Dragon Masters, and a book on microbes. His daughter had calculus and algebra textbooks as well as books by Alexander Pushkin, Nikki Giovanni, Arundhati Roy, and Ta-Nehisi Coates. The children received a love of adventure, literature, and social critique from their mother. Their father had instilled in them an interest in mathematics and the sciences.

The Kalinga family was late to school, which meant that Dr. Kalinga would be very late to his meeting. They ran to the subway station and just as they arrived on the platform the train doors closed. Dr. Kalinga said a strong word in his native language. This word he never translated for his children so they figured it must be a strong word. Just then the train door opened again.

They ran into the car and immediately the doors closed behind them. The train jerked out of the station and the Kalinga family fell backward. The children's backpacks spilled their books onto the floor. Dr. Kalinga's briefcase popped open. His papers flew everywhere and chrono-plasm spilled onto the floor.

And then they were struck by the inevitable stench every New Yorker eventually faces but tries with all their strength to avoid – the smell of raw funk and unkempt humanity. *Now* the Kalinga's understood why the train car was empty. The smell belonged to Kenny.

"Dr. Kalinga," said Kenny, the man stained with deep funk.

"Do I know you," replied Dr. Kalinga.

"I did not expect your children to be with you. I only brought one change of clothes." Kenny tried to give the funky smelling clothes to Dr. Kalinga who put the children behind him to protect them from this perceived mad man. "You do not understand. I am Dr. Kenneth Olewulu."

"Kenny!?" exclaimed Dr. Kalinga.

"Yes! Your newest theory is true," said Kenny.

"The chronoplasm works! But there are side effects. There is little time. Put these clothes on."

Yolo said, "But these clothes smell foul!"

"Naturally," said Kenny. "The raw scent will protect you during the transformation and it keeps other passengers from boarding. Time travel is not for everyone."

Gigi asked, "Do you mean that every homeless person who takes a car to themselves due to their smell is a time traveler?"

Kenny said, "No, my dear. Only some of them."

They noticed the train car was changing. It had somehow separated from the other cars and was increasing in speed through the subway.

"This is the effect of the chronoplasm. Now change into these clothes!" He gave Dr. Kalinga a set of funky clothes and he gave the children the clothes he was wearing.

"Father," said Gigi. "Must we?"

"I'm afraid so, my love. Dr. Olewulu was my doctoral adviser in physics and research partner in the early days of my work." He then turned to look directly at Kenny but continued to talk to his children. "Although this is completely un-orthodox, I trust Kenny." The Kalingas put on the dirty garments and the train car hit light speed. At that point Kenny disintegrated. Without the clothes he wasn't protected. Because the clothes were insufficient the family also changed. Their intellect radically increased in cognitive reasoning and their imagination deepened and expanded.

Dr. Kalinga said, "I now understand what Einstein meant when he said, 'Imagination is more important than knowledge. For knowledge is limited.'"

It was then that their adventures in time travel began. Yet they were limited in the scope of their travel. They could only travel through New York City train lines. The furthest back in time they could travel was October 9, 1863, the day train operation began. And the furthest into the future they could travel was the day the last piece of track decayed in the ruins of the subway system that existed under old New York.

* * *

"THE UNIVERSE IS AN ATOM."

Thoughtful Thelonious had a rough morning. He stayed up late secretly reading the Darth Vader graphic novel. He liked Darth Vader and even had sympathy for the dark overlord. Thelonious once reasoned to his dad, "Vader wants to do what is right, especially for his children. He just made some wrong life choices."

Since Thelonious didn't sleep much he was slow to get out of bed, slow to get dressed, and slow to brush his teeth. By the time he got to the breakfast table his eggs were cold and his toast was hard. And worse, he felt like his parents were rushing him to get ready for school. His mood deepened. He snapped at his parents and provoked his big sister, Thelma.

When they arrived at the Jefferson stop to catch the L train they just missed their train. Thelonious and Thelma started to fight. Their dad gave them a serious stink eye which they knew meant they needed to act right. The train arrived and the children got a seat. Dad had to stand. Thelma opened her math workbook and did long division exercises. Thelonious looked out the window into nothingness and wondered why there are windows on a train that never goes outside. He looked deeper into the void and imagined Darth Vader in heavy armor and helmet wielding his red light saber. He could almost hear the sound of the saber swooshing.

Thelma put her math book in her backpack and held Thelonious' hand. Although still sulking some, he welcomed his sister's touch, but did not turn to her. He continued looking through the window into the blackness. He imagined stars and solar systems and galaxies. His imagination went to the ends of the universe.

And beyond.

He imagined that our entire universe is but a small part of a tip of a toe nail on a little girl's foot. He imagined that she was made up of universes. He imagined her whole world made up of infinite universes. And then he imagined that her universe was merely an eyelash on an angel in another world.

Thelma asked, "What are you thinking about, Thelo?"

Thelonious turned to his sister, still holding her hand, and said, "The whole universe is an atom."

Dad, ever listening, poked in, "Sometimes letting your soul dwell deep lifts the spirit." They made their stop. Dad grabbed the children's hands. "We won't be early, but we'll be right on time," he said.

And the little girl in the other world put on beautiful glittery slippers and the angel batted his eyelashes. And all was right in the universes.

* * *

BROOKLYN TAMALE

Every morning Alma awoke early and made her way toward the Flushing Avenue M stop. She was very pregnant, but needed to sell tamales. She set up her tamale cart near the entrance to the station. She had a small pushcart, a blue cooler filled with tamales, an orange Igloo cooler filled with hot chocolate, a foldable chair, and an oversized rainbow umbrella. She set up early to sell to the laborers and construction workers first, and then to families with school children. On sunny days the umbrella served as a parasol protecting her from the sun. But this morning it was drizzly and the umbrella kept her from getting wet.

"Spicy chicken," said Hugo. Hugo was a hipster who caught the hipster trend when it was on its way out. His skinny jeans were uncomfortable for him to wear and perhaps more uncomfortable for others to see him wear. He was not a small man. In fact, he was rather husky.

"Would you like a napkin and fork?" asked Alma. She knew Hugo never took the napkin and fork, but she felt obliged to offer every patron the full service of her tamale cart.

"Your tamales are the best," said Hugo as he savored every bite.

"I'll tell you a secret," said Alma. "My grandma gets the credit for the high quality of these tamales. When she first showed me how to make them I wanted to make many tamales to make more money. Because my aim was to make money, some of the tamales were poor quality. My grandma inspected every tamale and threw out all that didn't meet her high standard. She said the tamales represent her, our family, and our heritage. Now I make only the best tamales, but every morning my grandma still inspects each tamale. She hardly throws out any now."

A mother with three children stopped at the tamale stand. Alma quickly gave them four tamales and said, "Running late, mami? Don't worry. Here's breakfast. Now hurry and make that train."

The mother said, "Alma, you're a life-saver!" and then she grabbed the tamales and her children and ran to catch the train. Alma's tamales were sold out!

"Another successful morning," said Hugo. Hugo liked to stand around the tamale cart and watch the people, even if it was raining a little. His only plan for the day was to go to a café, drink coffee, and write a music review for a website.

Alma cried loudly, "It's coming!" Her baby was on the way. "Hugo, I need your help!" She gave him her address and instructed him to take her tamale cart to her home and give it to her grand-mother. Alma then called her husband and told him, "It's time!" He promised to meet her at the hospital. She walked to the platform, boarded the train, and was on her way to the hospital.

* * *

HEAVEN'S RUINS

The elders told stories that were passed to them by their parents and grandparents, stories of a world that long since passed. One such story began, "In ancient days our world was but a shadow of the world above. The world above has fallen into ruins. The temples are destroyed and the gods have vanished. We only remain, and we are but a remnant of that former glory."

Seeku, the youngest of the elders, recently returned from an expedition to the world above. All the people gathered to hear Seeku. This was more than a story.

This was a first-hand report from heaven's ruins.

He began, "There was a great storm of wind and water. All of the dust – all of it! – is gone.

There are no towers like in our stories, but there are structures. Much vegetation is growing and there are large animals of many kinds."

All the people hung on Seeku's every word. He was the first of his generation to ascend to the world above.

"The yellow fire still burns half the day and everything is very bright. When the fireball sets another ball all-white appears."

The elders listened silently and intently. The people ooh-ed and ahh-ed at Seeku's report.

"Lastly and most importantly," he continued, "I have met descendants of the gods. They seem to have lost their power and glory, but they are wonderful to behold. They are bronze-skinned. Their language is similar to ours. And they desire friendship."

The people applauded and shouted praises at the promise of new friendship and a new world.

One of the council members interrupted, "We permitted this expedition, but we must be careful. We must move slowly. The world above is dangerous."

Another elder shouted, "I agree. Those so-called

gods destroyed their world. We should want nothing to do with them."

A next elder shouted, "War! Let us storm heaven, destroy these children of the gods."

The people listened to the elders argue.

Only Seeku said, "Let's seek peace and build relationship."

The people were stirred and factions formed. Eventually the council elders agreed to retreat deeper underground. They shut down tunnels, and their stories about heaven's ruins became grim and ominous.

A small band chose to follow Seeku and while most of the people followed the elders to retreat deeper underground, Seeku's band went above ground and joined the remnant who lived in heaven's ruins.

* * *

BUSKER'S CARNIVALE

I didn't think the day could get any weirder after one of the dancers on the Q line shouted, "You all ready for showtime!" and then while spinning around a pole the dancer accidentally kicked a tourist in the shoulder. The tourist was fine apart from a feeling of offense because the dancer suggested that the tourist should have been more watchful. Some passengers silently agreed and one lady said under her breath, "He did say *Showtime*." Another older gentleman disagreed aloud to himself, "It was only time before one of those so-called showtime dancers hurt somebody."

As the tourist and showtime dancer bantered, a mariachi band started playing. The three mariachis wore sombreros and festive garb. One played guitar, another had an egg shaker, and they all sang. It just so happened that a quartet

** standards crooning R&B standards in

Storbakken

of elderly gentlemen crooning R&B standards in four-part harmony decided to start singing at the very same moment as the mariachi band began playing. And neither relented. There was fast-paced twelve-string guitars strumming, an egg shaker shaking, and mariachi singers singing a chorus all the while the quartet crooned an a capella version of Otis Redding's *Sittin' on the Dock of the Bay.*

At the next stop a kirtan of Hare Krishna devotees boarded the train singing the maha mantra with cartalas and tabla. The mariachis and R&B quartet stopped to watch the Hindu monks singing and dancing. As the Hindu monks sang, an open-air evangelist began thumping on the Bible. It was like some kind of strange spiritual battle between the Hindus and the Christian. The monks sang their mantras and the evangelist told the promises of the Good News and also the consequences of the bad news. At the next stop the monks and the evangelist got off.

The train was then boarded by a clown with a big red nose and rainbow wig and accompanied by a poodle in a tutu. They were followed by a second group of showtime dancers, a person painted completely in silver, and a large West Indian man with a steel drum. As the train started

82

toward the next station, I arose from my seat and showcased my talent of impersonating wild animals. I growled deep like a lion, chirped like a flock of birds, and laughed like a chimpanzee. When I finished the whole train erupted in applause and laughter. We had arrived at Union Square for the Buskers' Carnavale.

❊ ❊ ❊

TEVIN'S TERRIBLE DAY

Ms. Hines' fourth grade class was crowded into the train car. Several of the children's parents were present to serve as chaperones.

The class of twenty-one students was broken up into five groups of four students with a chaperone assigned to each group. Ms. Hines had the group of five.

Tevin was in Ms. Hines' group.

It wasn't that Tevin was a bad kid. But you couldn't say he was a good kid either. Basically, he was a regular kid who felt deeply and sometimes reacted too quickly.

That morning Tevin's dad who ran a pet shop

told him that he had sold Tevin's favorite turtle.

And then while waiting for the train to school he got into a fight with Kevin, his big brother. Tevin had to use the bathroom and when he told Kevin he had a bathroom emergency his big brother laughed at him. Tevin pushed Kevin and the two started to fight on the platform. And then a big man shouted at them, "Hey jackasses, knock it off."

They bumped into a little girl when wrestling so they knew it was definitely time to quit, but Tevin was still fuming.

On top of that, Tevin pooped a little during the tussle.

And now he was assigned to Ms. Hines' group. All the other groups had four kids, but his group had five kids. He knew that he was the fifth kid, the odd one out. All the children were paired up, Tevin was paired with Ms. Hines.

So there stood Tevin on the R train, clothes dirty from the tussle with his brother, a tiny poop stain in his pants, no turtle to return home to, and he had to stand next to the teacher the whole day. His day couldn't get any worse.

Or could it?

The train was moving.

Tevin watched two men banter loudly as he thought about the fight earlier with Kevin. As the men got louder he noticed the emergency break cord hanging from the ceiling. He always wanted to pull it. It just hung there with one single purpose – to be pulled. In that moment as he watched the men banter and thought about the fight with Kevin he just wanted it all to stop – the men bantering, standing next to the teacher, his dirty clothes, all of it – and for no good reason he pulled the cord.

The train jerked to a stop and everyone lurched forward. The train stopped for a long time.

Tevin stood still and remained quiet. Ms. Hines stayed close to Tevin. She knew she would have to call his parents to tell them about the incident, but she knew that in that moment Tevin needed someone to stand with him and not be angry with him but to simply let him know that he would be okay.

Finally, the class made it to their destination – the Hayden Planetarium. They looked at moon rocks and meteors, but it wasn't until they entered the planetarium that Tevin found peace.

The students entered the space show and Tevin was struck by a sense of awe and wonder as the narrator waxed poetic about stars and galaxies and the universe. Tevin lost himself in the grandeur of all being. He joined with the mystery and beauty of the cosmos.

That sense of wonder stayed with Tevin all the way back to school, and even further until he met up again with Kevin and they rode the train home together.

Peace followed Tevin, but only for so long.

It had rained earlier in the day. As Tevin and Kevin walked toward home a big truck drove through a puddle and splashed the two brothers, soaking their clothes.

When they walked through the door of their home, their parents were sitting at the kitchen table. "Boys, come have a seat. There's something we need to discuss with you."

Jason Storbakken

* * *

TURTLE FAMILY

"**M**ama Turtle, tell us the story of how you and Daddy Turtle met."

"Oh Daughter Turtle, haven't you heard that story too many times?"

Daughter and Brother Turtle pleaded, "Plee-eeease."

Mama Turtle began, "Quite a while ago when I was a young turtle I was exploring an abandoned subway tunnel and I found a scroungy little turtle laid out flat on his shell. I drew close and smelled how funky your daddy was. Now in those days he was not the handsome turtle he is today. Nor was he wise or very kind.

"I walked over to this turtle and asked if he needed any help getting right side up. That little turtle had the nerve to say, 'I don't need any help.' Well, I grab a seat in a ray of sunshine peaking through a crack in the ceiling and watch this turtle squirm and struggle to no avail. Finally, this turtle with the sass mouth says, 'What are you gonna do? Just sit there and watch? Why don't you help me out?' I say, 'Gladly, but first you have to tell me how you got yourself in this predicament.' Finally, with many sighs and ughs he told me his story."

"'I used to live with my moms and pops in the Bronx River. And ended up in a pet shop in Soho. It wasn't so bad. The shopkeeper's son visited me every day. But when the shopkeeper found out that I'm a snapping turtle he decided to get rid of me. So he dumped me in a sewage drain one rainy day and I ended up here – flat on my back.'

"In those days your daddy had a hard shell but he was soft inside. He didn't trust folks too much and for good reason – he had been stolen as a baby, abandoned, and treated like trash. With much effort, I helped turn him right side up. And the rest is history."

* * *

HIP HOP HAT

Tavis and his dad were on their way out of the house when Tavis' mom said, "Wait! I bought a hat for you at the Brooklyn Flea. Wear it to the birthday party!"

Tavis tried on the oversized, fitted baseball cap.

"It's hip hop," said Tavis' dad.

Tavis liked fashion, but at times he could be self-conscious. He hesitated to wear the hip hop hat, but after some persuasion by his parents he relented and wore the hat.

They walked down Fulton Street toward the train. Vendors said, "Looking cool, little man." A bodega clerk stepped outside his store to tell Tavis, "Stay fresh, b-boy!" Tavis' dad smiled. But Tavis didn't appreciate all the unwarranted attention.

When they stepped into the train Tavis said to his dad, "There's something going on with this hat."

Dad said, "People like it. That's all."

"No, dad. There's *something* going on with *this* hat."

There was energy surging through him. The hat had power and the power had overtaken him. Like thunder in the heavens, Tavis heard a mighty voice say, "The power of hip hop compels thee." And all of a sudden Tavis was on his feet spittin' hip hop rhymes.

"Follow me into a solo, get in the flow/And you can picture like a photo/Music mix, mellow maintains to make/Melodies for emcees, motivates the breaks/I'm everlasting, I can go on for days and days/With rhyme displays that engrave deep as x-rays/I can take a phrase that's rarely heard/Flip it – now it's a daily word."

At that Tavis sat down. His dad looked at him astounded. "What do you know about Eric B. and Rakim?" Tavis took the hat off, looked inside and read a handwritten tag, "Property of Africa Bambaataa, Universal Zulu Nation. The One Who Wears This Hat Will Have The Power of Hip Hop."

Tavis' dad was in disbelief. He tried the hat on and like his son he heard the heavenly thunder, "The power of hip hop compels thee." And he was on his feet.

"I'm alone but my tone is a sharp tune/Developing pictures in your brain like a darkroom/Rappers are captured and tortured with rapture/ In 3-D is a G coming at you."

And then he returned to his seat next to Tavis.

A man with salt-and-pepper hair nodded to Tavis' dad and said, "Kool G Rap."

The other passengers were amazed at the father-son hip hop duo they had just witnessed. Tavis and his dad got off the train and went to the birthday party.

The hat disturbed Tavis' reserved nature so when he arrived at the party he passed the hip hop hat forward to the birthday girl and with great joy and deep relief said, "Happy Birthday, Lil Nat!"

Jason Storbakken

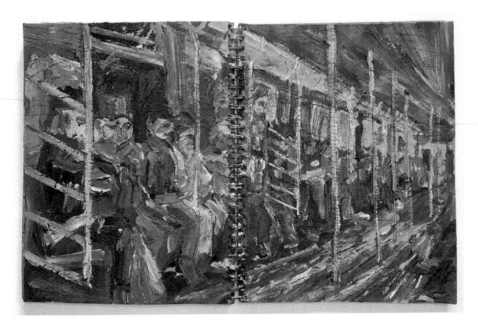

* * *

LAST STOP ON THE Z TRAIN

E arth was on the brink of annihilation. Worm holes opened in the sky and fleets of extragalactic spaceships entered the earth's atmosphere, darkening the heavens. New Yorkers unglued themselves from their screens to look upward.

Beneath the surface of humanity's collective consciousness, battles were brewing among mystical creatures on earth and an all-out war was waging just beyond their galaxy for millennia.

The deep quiet that lingered over the mass of awe-struck people was broken by a businessman's shriek of terror.

Madness ensued.

At that moment, the most peculiar looking train emerged from the portal. It was Dr. Kalinga and his children, Gigi and Yolo. They also had Seeku and his band of followers with him.

Everyone was in shock, except for two people – who were not humans, but were humanoid. Occlo and Capac were space tourists, albeit unauthorized. They received a message earlier that day that warned of General Isab's imminent invasion of Earth. They were making their way to the last stop on the Z train, which served as the location of the portal to their home-world.

Occlo and Capac were on the Z train and almost at the last stop when General Isab emitted an electromagnetic pulse, causing all technology and machines to cease operating. Occlo and Capac exited the train and ran toward the portal.

Occlo arrived first and attempted to jump through the portal, but the pulse had also closed all wormholes and portals. Occlo hit his head on the wall, fell to the ground and died. Capac looked at Occlo with great grief and said, "Beep blop click bloooopity calack," which translates to, "Don't leave me! You must have one more life in you. Please!"

Occlo and Capac were from a species that allowed each person to regenerate seven times. Unfortunately, Occlo had no lives left.

Mrs. Miller, a tourist from Iowa, ran to Occlo to see if she might help. She was a registered nurse. She began to administer CPR, pressing on his chest. As she attempted to resuscitate Occlo, Capac cried, "Mocla shokla ballu clack plop!" which translates as "Why are you crushing his privies!" Mrs. Miller did not know that this species' lungs are located in their toes.

Dr. Kalinga noticed the CPR wasn't working so he interjected with a defibrillator, but due to the pulse it didn't charge. All hope for Occlo seemed lost. He turned to the gathered crowd and spoke: "I have traveled through time and space, and sadly this day is the start of humanity's extinction. The world is in a loop and as often as I travel to this point in time destruction is always imminent. This time, I have brought with me Seeku, one of the last humans. He comes from a world beyond ours. He is witness to our future ruined state."

Seeku did not address the crowd. Instead, he looked at Occlo and Capac and intuitively understood their nature. He communicates with heart-language – not words, but empathic communication. He expressed to Capac, "I understand your species' gift of rebirth. Might you give one of your lives so that your beloved might live?"

Capac understood. She went deep within her inner person and mustered great hope and courage from a wellspring that was in her but also beyond her, a wellspring that connected her to a river of life that linked all sentient beings, and which ultimately poured into and drew from the original source, an ocean of shared consciousness that ebbs and flows through the multiverses like breath.

Capac breathed from this place, and a great cosmic shift began. Occlo was restored to life. In fact, all of his lives were replenished as well. And together, their shared wellspring overflowed into all other lives. Where there once was sorrow, despair, and fear, there was now joy, hope, and courage.

This wellspring moved like a wave across the worlds and galaxies, until the multiverses were born anew, emerging from the husk of the old world into a new world.

* * *

CONTRIBUTORS

Jason Storbakken is an Anabaptist minister and author of "Radical Spirituality: Repentance, Resistance, Revolution" (Orbis) and the forthcoming "Bowery Mission: Grit and Grace on Manhattan's Oldest Street" (Plough). These 23 stories in LAST STOP ON THE Z TRAIN were first told to his children as they rode the subway.

Pairoj Pichetmetakul is a Buddhist monk-turned-street artist. His work aims to shift public perception and cultivate compassion. One of his current projects consists of riding every subway car on the MTA and painting the images and visions he sees from the 1 train to the Z train.

Special thanks to artist Allie Wilkinson who contributed the painting, "Abuela". And Chloe Storbakken who first told the story, "I'm not staring. I'm smelling."